The extraordinary tales of
Queenie Alice Moon

The Shooting Star

Jo Brothers
Illustrated by Lovee

The Extraordinary Tales of Queenie Alice Moon - The Shooting Star

Second Printing, 2015
Text and Artwork Copyright © 2015 Jo Brothers
ISBN 978-0-9922538-7-5

Published by:
Perpetuity Media
PO Box 4444
Shortland Street
Auckland
New Zealand 1140

www.perpetuitymedia.com

Published in New Zealand

Printed in the United States of America

Everyone has
extraordinary tales to tell.

This book is dedicated to
you.

Queenie Alice Moon and her parents King Leo and Queen Arabella, lived in the land of Spectrum, a magical Kingdom on Earth. Spectrum was deeply connected to the stars and the moon.

A land of rich colours and light, deep blue oceans, green fields and beautiful pink and red flowers in lush gardens, where you could find pink bears, blue and yellow butterflies, yellow and black bumble bees and flower fairies.

Queenie had several magical guardians including a golden dragon named Yang who had golden scales made from pure sunshine.

Queenie had magical Angelic powers and a Crown of Wisdom to always feel the truth because sometimes the heart feels what is invisible to the eyes.

In fact that is how she met Moonbeam the Unicorn. One day when Queenie was out in the Crimson Valley she saw a baby unicorn being attacked by evil flying snakes.

Queenie immediately ran to protect Moonbeam, they became instant friends and Moonbeam was made a royal unicorn guardian to look after Queenie.

Queenie Alice Moon's parents, King Leo and Queen Arabella worked for the Heavenly Government that protected Earth and all the realms with 101 undercover Angels.

Leo and Arabella were the guardians of the Akashic records library which was located in the sky castles of the Upper Worlds. The Akashic library is where all the past, present and future history of all Worlds are kept.

Leo & Arabella Moon had been undercover Angels since before Queenie was born and they had taken an oath to protect Earth and all the Worlds and Kingdoms from an army of evil flying snakes, to ensure there was the correct balance of love, kindness and light on Earth.

Leo and Arabella were often summoned by the Heavenly Government to attend the assembly of Angels to receive their next assignment. So they were very grateful to have Moonbeam and Yang as official royal guardians who would look after Queenie when they were away.

Queenie and her parents lived in a magical Palace with hundreds of rooms of all shapes and sizes, there were ballrooms, bedrooms, magic rooms, turrets, tunnels and attics.

One of Queenie's favourite rooms was the replenishment kitchen and its sweet treats. Every time you picked up a lovely cake treat to eat, another cake would appear to replace it. Moonbeam and Yang both had a sweet tooth and would often sneak down to the kitchen for a midnight treat.

Queenie loved to read books and particularly loved to read all about the stars, the moon, the planets and astrological movements.

One of Queenie Alice Moon's favourite things that she liked to do, as she waited for a shooting star, was to watch and talk to the stars and the moon in the darkness of the night. The stars showered Queenie in stardust and the crescent moon sang her lullabies.

Queenie did not need a telescope to see the shooting stars because when she talked to the stars they would move closer. A shooting star is a sign that great positive change is about to happen in all the Worlds and Kingdoms.

On the nights when Queenie saw a shooting star she and Yang would dance in circles of happiness.

Queenie loved the full moon as this was when she was allowed to receive a surprise gift. Sometimes the gift was for Queenie herself and sometimes it was for her to share.

Queenie was allowed to go to the east wing to choose a door to open. The east wing rooms of the castle were all filled with magic, secrets and treasure and behind each door was a different gift.

Queenie and Yang were lying on the roof of the castle as the divine yellow moon rose full and bright on the fifteenth day of the month.

Queenie felt very excited saying, "Yang! Its now time for me to choose a door to open and to reveal new opportunities". Queenie had dreamt that something amazing would happen this full moon and she knew that a dream was like a letter to your soul.

Queenie jumped onto Yang's back, they flew over the Palace rooftops and in through an open window, down to the east wing where doors of different colours glowed brightly.

Queenie jumped off Yang's back and stood beside him looking down a long passage of doors. "So many different doors to choose from!" said Queenie excitedly.

Queenie trusted her instincts and felt herself being attracted to the red door. She stood in front of the red door with stars and opened the door, not knowing what to expect.

When she saw what was behind the red door, a huge smile lit up her face and warmed her heart.

Queenie bent down to pick up the cutest regal Pug puppy she had ever seen. "Pugnatius is my name, never let me go, never let me go!", the Pug puppy said as he smiled. "Pugnatius you are the friend I have wished for. I wished for you on a shooting star, and here you are!" Queenie said excitedly, hugging Pugnatius.

Friends are more precious than treasure, they are always there for us and we are always there for them.

Sometimes we know each other better than we know ourselves.

About Jo

Jo has a passion for storytelling and writing that started when she was a young girl and continues to this very day. She has a vivid imagination and loves creating new worlds and wonderful characters that burst into life with valour and flamboyance such as Queenie Alice Moon and Nano the Robot.

She equally writes intriguing novelettes with quirky, eccentric characters that are weaved into supernatural themes and in her soon to be released book series Immortales Excelsus she writes about an ordinary, thoroughly bored teen, Sabra Leon, who discovers she and her family are not so ordinary and that their history has more than a few secrets that date back to the dawn of time.

"Thanks for visiting, happy imagining!"

Please keep in touch with me at www.jobrothers.com

Jo lives in Auckland, New Zealand with her husband Sean, in a home filled with books and imagination.